When a Dragon Meets a Baby

First published 2021 by Nosy Crow Ltd
The Crow's Nest, 14 Baden Place
Crosby Row, London SE1 1YW
www.nosycrow.com

ISBN 978 1 78800 888 4 (HB)
ISBN 978 1 78800 889 1 (PB)

Nosy Crow and associated logos are trademarks
and/or registered trademarks of Nosy Crow Ltd.

Text © Caryl Hart 2021
Illustrations © Rosalind Beardshaw 2021

A CIP catalogue record for this book is available from the British Library.

Printed in China

Papers used by Nosy Crow are made from wood grown in sustainable forests.

10 9 8 7 6 5 4 3 2 1 (HB)
10 9 8 7 6 5 4 3 2 1 (PB)

For Jess –
the best big sister
anywhere xx
C. H.

To my babies,
Freddie and Iris x
R. B.

When a Dragon Meets a Baby

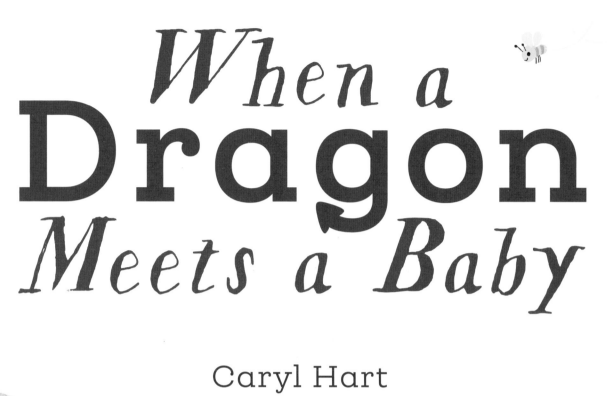

Caryl Hart
Rosalind Beardshaw

 nosy crow

When a **dragon's** parents say,

"Our baby has come home today!" . . .

. . . does she refuse to say hello,
or grumble, "Why?"
or "Baby GO!"?

Why, no! Dragons don't do that!

A dragon stands on tippy-toes
to kiss that tiny baby's nose,
then finds a **squishy** snuggle bug –
the sort that babies **love** to hug –
and says, "Hi, Baby! Here you go."

A dragon's **kind** like that, you know.

Then, if the baby's bottom's wet,
this **clever** dragon's quick to get
the nappies and the changing mat.

She finds a nice clean vest and hat
while Daddy gets the baby dressed.

This dragon really **is** the best!

When relatives or friends pop by,
does this young dragon **huff** and **sigh**?

And does she bellow, "Play with me," or pester Mummy endlessly?

Why, no! Dragons don't do that!

She shows the guests the baby's things –
the buggy and the teething rings –
then unwraps every toy and book
and gives them to the baby, "Look!"
She says each present is just right.

A little dragon's SO polite.

Then, while her mummy has a doze,
this sweet, **kind-hearted** dragon knows
to help with tidying the house.

Then, quiet as a little mouse,
she reads with Daddy happily.

A dragon's **thoughtful** as can be.

Next, at the baby's feeding time,
does this small dragon **moan** or **whine**?

And does she say that Mummy's knee
is where **she** is supposed to be?

Why, no! Dragons don't do that!

She brings a most delicious treat –
the kind that mummy dragons eat –
and when they've all enjoyed their snack,
this dragon pats the baby's back
to soothe that poppet's hiccupping.

A dragon helps with everything!

Then in the bath, a dragon's **kind** –
if Baby splashes, **she** won't mind.

She shares her favourite sailing boat
and lets her yellow ducklings float
around the baby's tiny feet.

Yes, dragons **really** are that sweet!

But if the baby starts to howl,
that's when a dragon might well growl!

Then you must hold her close and say,
"You've been a **perfect** help today!
The best big sister **anywhere**."

A dragon **knows** her mummy cares.

At last, when Baby's tucked up tight,
all ready for a peaceful night,

do dragons **bash** and **crash** their toys
and make an awful lot of noise?

Why, no! Dragons don't do that!

She helps her mummy rock the cot
and check the baby's not too hot,
then sings a gentle lullaby
and **whispers**,
"Baby, hush, don't cry,"
then tiptoes silently away.

That's just how **dragons** end the day.

And if, when **she** should be asleep,
this dragon starts to wail and weep,
"I want my **baby**," down the hall,

well...

she is a dragon after all!